Germany

Russia

Poland

France

Korea

Iran

Japan

Iraq

China

India

Laos

Indonesia

Zimbabwe

GLASS SLIPPER, GOLD SANDAL

A WORLDWIDE CINDERELLA

PAUL FLEISCHMAN

Illustrated by JULIE PASCHKIS

HENRY HOLT AND COMPANY NEW YORK

For Flannery
—P. F.

To Reka Simonsen,
who gives me such interesting shoes to try on
—J. P.

Henry Holt and Company, LLC
Publishers since 1866
175 Fifth Avenue
New York, New York 10010
mackids.com

Henry Holt® is a registered trademark of Henry Holt and Company, LLC.
Text copyright © 2007 by Paul Fleischman
Illustrations copyright © 2007 by Julie Paschkis
Library of Congress Cataloging-in-Publication Data
Fleischman, Paul.
Glass slipper, gold sandal: a worldwide Cinderella / Paul Fleischman; illustrated by Julie Paschkis.—1st ed.
p.   cm.
Summary: The author draws from a variety of folk traditions to put together this version of Cinderella,
including elements from Mexico, Iran, Korea, Russia, Appalachia, and more.
ISBN 978-0-8050-7953-1
[1. Folklore.] I. Cinderella. English. II. Paschkis, Julie, ill. III. Title.
PZ8.F5766Gl 2007   398.2—dc22   [E]   2006030615

First Edition—2007 / Designed by Laurent Linn
The artist used Winsor & Newton gouaches to create the illustrations for this book.
Printed in China by RR Donnelley Asia Printing Solutions Ltd., Dongguan City, Guangdong Province.

AUTHOR'S NOTE

A chameleon changes color to match its surroundings. Stories do the same. The earliest recorded Cinderella tale is thought to date from ninth-century China. Traveling across the globe, it changed its clothes but not its essence. Rivalry, injustice, and the dream of wrongs righted are universal, no matter our garments. When the story reached France, it acquired the glass slippers and coachmen-mice familiar to Western readers. More than a thousand other versions are known. I pictured a book that would let us listen in on the tale-tellers we don't often hear, who've breathed this story to life around fires of peat and piñon pine, swinging in hammocks and snuggling under deerskins. I'm especially indebted to Judy Sierra's fine collection, *Cinderella* (Oryx Press, 1992).

ONCE UPON A TIME there lived a wealthy merchant whose wife had died. They had one daughter, gentle-eyed and good-hearted.

Down the road lived a widow with two daughters. The woman gave the girl treats when she passed—*pan dulce* to eat, sugarcane to chew. The girl knew that her father was lonely. "You should marry the widow," she told him. "She's nice to me." The father had his doubts, but the girl kept asking—and how long can a father say no to his daughter?

MEXICO

And so, he and the widow were married.

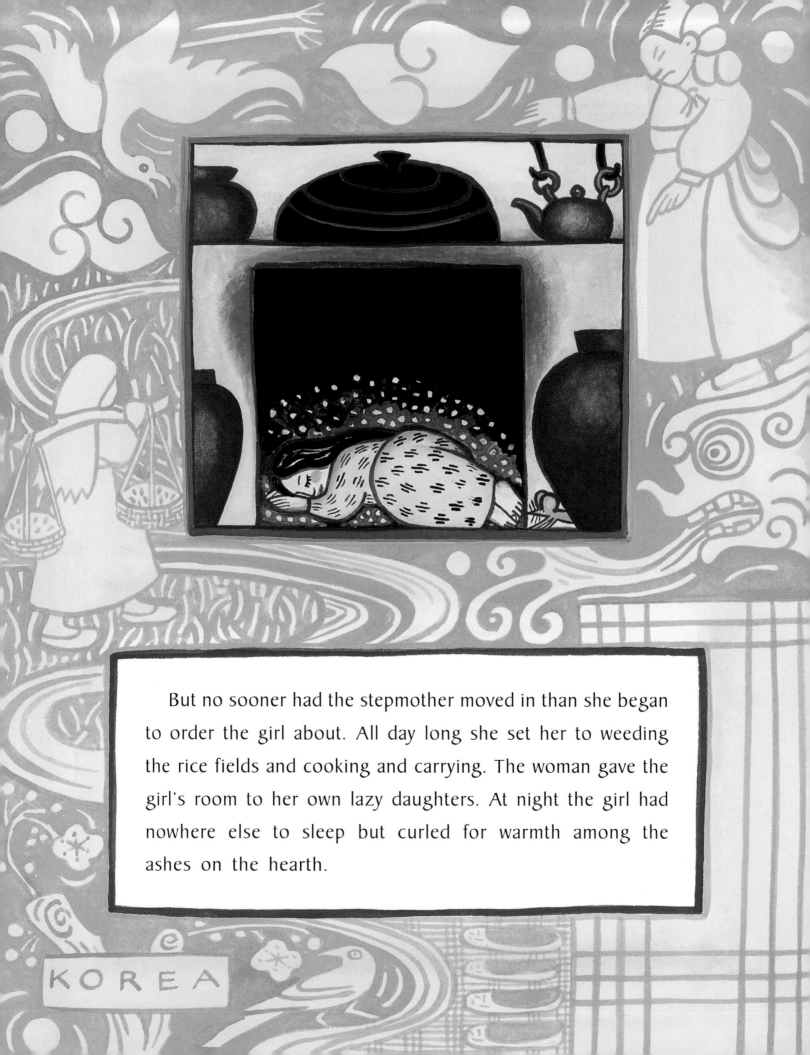

But no sooner had the stepmother moved in than she began to order the girl about. All day long she set her to weeding the rice fields and cooking and carrying. The woman gave the girl's room to her own lazy daughters. At night the girl had nowhere else to sleep but curled for warmth among the ashes on the hearth.

KOREA

Her stepmother allowed her only a few scraps of food. Her stomach howled. Then the girl recalled how she'd begged her father to marry. "I picked up the scorpion with my own hand," she told herself. She vowed not to complain to her father and upset him.

IRAQ

RUSSIA

But when the girl was out tending the cattle, the beasts heard her crying for hunger. "Don't weep," said one of the cows. And the animal poured honey for her from its horn . . .

IRAN

. . . and a fairy gave her figs and apricots . . .

. . . and Godfather Snake gave her rice.

INDIA

Once she was eating well and proper, the girl bloomed into a right rare beauty. The stepmother couldn't fathom it. And meanwhile her own sour-faced daughters would curdle the milk if they looked at it twice.

IRELAND

One day it was announced far and wide that the Great King was in search of a queen. All the unmarried women dressed in their finest robes and set off for the palace.

ZIMBABWE

To make sure the girl couldn't go, the stepmother threw an apronful of lentils into the ashes and ordered her to pick them all out.

GERMANY

"And scour all the kitchen pots, too!" she hollered.

APPALACHIA

As soon as the stepmother left with her daughters, the girl burst into tears. Outside, the sparrows heard her. In they flew and pecked the lentils from the ashes.

GERMANY

Then a witch woman came in and spoke a spell—and up jumped the pots and scoured themselves.

APPALACHIA

The girl was free to go, but she had nothing to wear except rags. Then she looked in her mother's sewing basket.

LAOS

Then she reached into the hole in the birch tree.

RUSSIA

Then a crocodile swam up to the surface—and in its mouth was a sarong made of gold . . .

INDONESIA

. . . a cloak sewn of king-fisher feathers . . .

CHINA

. . . a kimono red as sunset.

JAPAN

FRANCE

And on the girl's feet appeared a pair of glass slippers . . .

INDIA

. . . diamond anklets . . .

IRAQ

. . . sandals of gold.

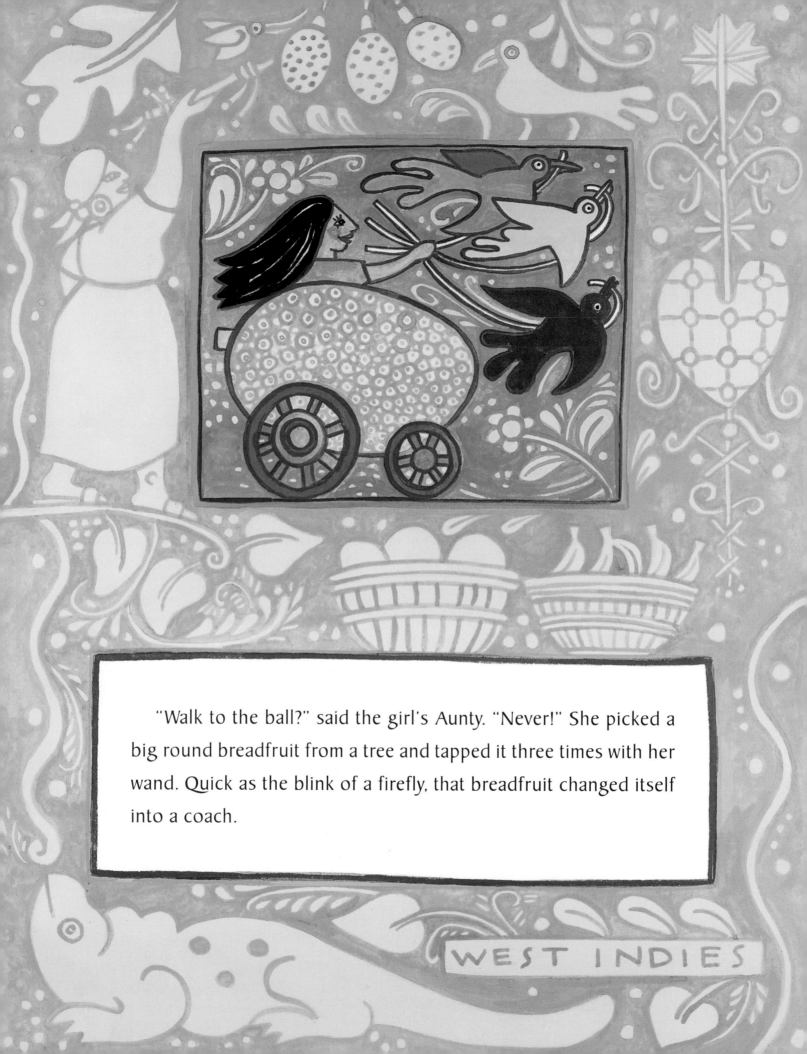

"Walk to the ball?" said the girl's Aunty. "Never!" She picked a big round breadfruit from a tree and tapped it three times with her wand. Quick as the blink of a firefly, that breadfruit changed itself into a coach.

WEST INDIES

When she made her entrance, so great was her beauty that the musicians stopped playing.

POLAND

No one, not even her stepmother, knew who the beautiful stranger was.

INDONESIA

All night the girl danced with the headman's son, until the first rooster crowed. Then she remembered—she had to leave at once.

She leaped onto her mare's golden saddle. "Who *are* you?" called the prince. The girl had no time for words and charged down the lane. The prince sprinted beside her, got a hand on her shoe—and the dainty thing pulled off in his fingers as she galloped away.

The King declared he would marry the golden shoe's owner. He ordered the women of the court to try it on, but none could squeeze inside it. And so he went searching for its owner, up and down mountains . . .

CHINA

IRAN

. . . and across the deserts . . .

LAOS

. . . until he came to the stepmother's house. When she saw him approach, she grabbed her stepdaughter, wrapped her in a mat, and hid her.

"I'm certain the shoe will fit one of my fine-favored girls," said the woman. Grunting and sweating, her older daughter tried to wrestle the shoe on, but couldn't. Neither could the younger.

FRANCE

Just then, a rooster began to crow:

*"They put the ugly one on show
And hid the beauty down below."*

IRAQ

The girl was brought forward. "Don't waste your time with that one," said the stepmother. But the magistrate looked into the girl's eyes, took the straw sandal in his hand—and slipped it onto her foot with ease.

She and the Great King were married at the palace, where the guests feasted on mangoes and melons . . .

ZIM·BAB·WE

INDIA

. . . rice seasoned with almonds . . .

IRELAND

. . . beef stew and lamb stew . . .

. . . anise cookies and custards.

MEXICO

Such a wedding it was, and such an adoring couple . . .

IRAQ

. . . and such a wondrous turn of events . . .

KOREA

. . . that people today are still telling the story.

Ireland ⊙

Appalachia ⊙

Mexico ⊙

West Indies ⊙